A COOKED-UP FAIRY TALE

Penny Parker Klostermann

illustrated by Ben Mantle

Random House 🏠 New York

Library of Congress Cataloging-in-Publication Data is available upon request.
ISBN 978-1-101-93232-2 (trade) — ISBN 978-1-101-93233-9 (lib. bdg.) — ISBN 978-1-101-93234-6 (ebook)

Book design by Nicole de las Heras

MANUFACTURED IN CHINA
10 9 8 7 6 5 4 3 2 1
First Edition

With love for my sisters, Tris, Cari & Janna
—P.P.K.

For Mia Mei Carlyle
—B.M.

Although William lived in the magical land of fairy tales, he preferred pastries to princesses, kitchens to kingdoms, and recipes to the *Royal Reporter*.

William dreamed of being a chef—
a chef known throughout the land.

Whether sautéed, sifted, basted,
or baked, puréed, poached,
filleted, or flaked,

William's dishes
were perfect.

But cooking *happily ever*
was a different story.

He'd tried working at the Brick House.

But the menu was too dangerous.

Pot-o'-Wolf Stew
Bring water to a boil.
Stir in 3 cups peas,
3 cups carrots,
3 cups potatoes.
Add 1 Big Bad Wolf.

Too cold!

He'd served up porridge at Three Bears Bistro.

Too hot!

But folks there were very persnickety.

And he'd baked for Gingerbread-on-the-Go.
That hadn't ended well, either.

William decided he'd better cook from home, but his pantry
was almost bare. So he emptied the last few coins from his cookie
jar and headed to the market.

To: Judy, Chief of
Fairy-Tale Headquarters

FAIRY-TALE FOOD

MUST DELIVER
FOR BEDTIME

"What's this?" asked William.
"Fairy-tale food? Must be splendid!"

But it was only raw apples . . . beans . . . and a pumpkin.

"This isn't splendid," said William. "Clearly, Fairy-Tale Headquarters needs a good chef to spice things up before the bedtime delivery."

So he sliced and diced,

chopped and topped,

and stirred and whirred.

Then he packed up his delectable creations and followed the signs to Fairy-Tale Headquarters.

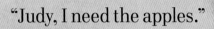

"Judy, I need the apples."

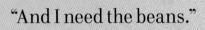

"And I need the beans."

"The pumpkin, Judy,
the pumpkin."

"Where can that delivery be?"
asked Judy, in a stew.

"I believe I can help," said William. "May I present—

Baked Apples with Caramel Drizzle,

Bean Soup with Smoked Ham,

and Pumpkin Pie with Cream and Candied Pecans!"

"Who—what—why?" stammered Judy. "I need shiny apples and raw beans and a whole pumpkin. Don't you know anything about fairy tales?"

"I'm sorry," said William. "I read cookbooks, not fairy tales. But maybe I could—"

"You? You've cooked up enough trouble!" said Judy. "It's bedtime and the tales must begin. Now leave . . . and take this book of fairy tales with you!"

William plopped down outside the kingdom wall and opened the book.

"Poisoned apple? Beanstalk? Pumpkin coach? Oh my!" said William. "Fairy tales really do have their own ingredients."

He rushed back to find Judy.

"Did I spoil the apple story?" he blurted out.

"'Snow White'? Actually, she loved your baked apples and ate every one.

"She was so stuffed that she fell into a deep sleep. Of course, this caused a stir with those seven dwarfs.

"But then there was a passing prince.
And a kiss. So . . . *happily ever after.*"

"Thank goodness," said William.
"And the beans story?"

"'Jack and the Beanstalk'? The giant said something like
'Fee, fi, fo, fum, I smell soup and I want me some.'

"Jack was in a pickle, but he drove a hard bargain and traded the pot of soup for the giant's castle in the clouds. . . . Another *happily ever after.*"

SOLD

"Such a relief," said William. "What about the pumpkin tale?"

"'Cinderella'? It's still unfolding. We'll find out together."

"Oh no!" said William. "This is a recipe for disaster."

Then . . .

Slip!

Flip!

Whack!

Smack!

"Scrumptious!" said the prince. "Simply delicious!"

He took another bite and said, "I vow to search all the land until I find . . .

the baker of this pie!"

Cinderella slumped in her puddle of pumpkin.

"This isn't *happily ever after*," sighed Judy.

"Happily ever after?" murmured William.

He strode right into the fairy tale.

"Your Highness, I baked the pie. And I will bake you pies ever after. But may I suggest you can have your pie and your princess, too?"

The prince gazed at Cinderella.
"You're a feast for my eyes," he said.
"Would you care to dance?"

"My, my," said Judy. "It looks like you've cooked up another happy ending."

And from that night forward, the prince and his princess ate like kings and queens, and William cooked *happily ever after.*